DON'T ASK
THE
DRAGON

LEMN SISSAY
&
GREG STOBBS

This is Alem. He's alone and it's his birthday.

He's wondering where he could call home.

Alem meets a bear and asks, 'where shall I go?'

Alem wanders on
and soon meets a fox.
He asks,
'Where shall I go?'

And the fox whispers
under his breath,
'I don't know!'

The bear told you.
I'm telling you too.
Just don't ask the dragon!

He will eat you!'

'How Strange!' Alem thought.

Alem asks everyone he meets,
'It's my birthday. Where shall I go?'

He asks

a meerkat

a treefrog

a fruitbat

and a bulldog.

'Just don't ask the dragon!

HE WILL EAT YOU!'

So the meerkat chases the treefrog.

And the treefrog chases the fruitbat.

And the fruitbat chases the bulldog.
And that is **THAT**.

Alem wandered on.

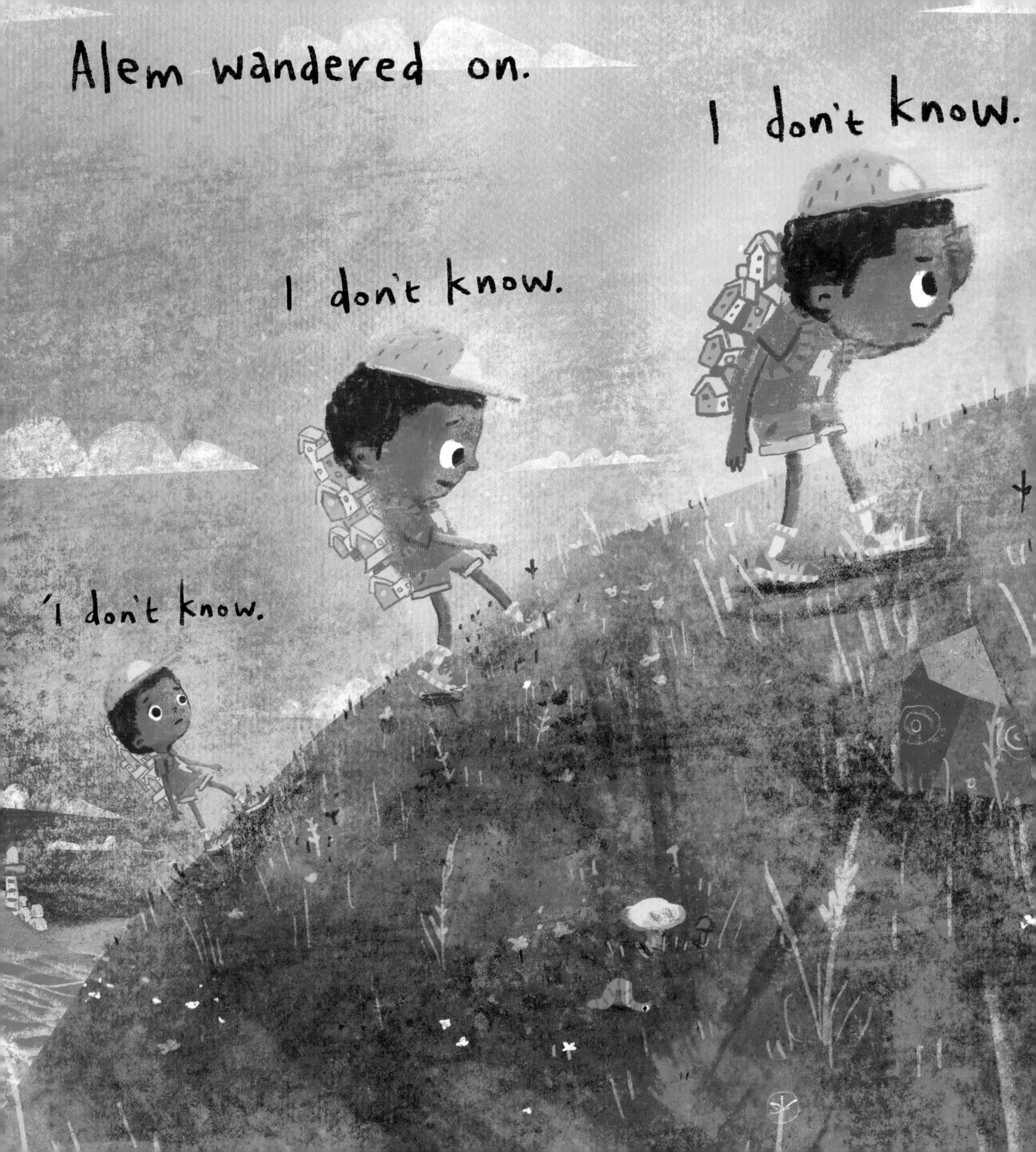

'I don't know.

I don't know.

I don't know.

with a pinch of basil

and rosemary too.

But I'm vegetarian.
I came from the sea.
I'm not going to eat you!
Will you stay for tea?

I am not just any dragon.
I'm the dragon of words.
Do you know what your name means?

Alem turned to the dragon and said,
'It's my birthday and I've asked
everyone, "where shall I go?"
and everyone has said, "I don't know."
Do you know?'

Now the dragon smiled his toothy grin.
...... 'You're in luck. I do!

There is a town
where the bravest go
And I have named it

I DON'T KNOW.

WELCOME TO
I DON'T KNOW

Alem's birthday song strikes up

with all his friends beside him.

He smiles and his face lights up.

Home was always inside him.

For our parents

First published in Great Britain, the USA and Canada
in 2022 by Canongate Books Ltd,
14 High Street, Edinburgh EH1 1TE

Distributed in the USA by Publishers Group West and
in Canada by Publishers Group Canada

canongate.co.uk

1

British Library Cataloguing-in-Publication Data
A catalogue record for this book is available on
request from the British Library

Hardback ISBN 978 1 83885 398 3
Paperback ISBN 978 1 83885 400 3

Artworking by Sharon McTeir, Creative Publishing Services

Printed and bound in Italy by LEGO S.p.A.

MIX
Paper from
responsible sources
FSC
www.fsc.org   FSC® C023419